The Madness of Emotions

Deepti Dogra

Think Tank™
Books

Title: The Madness of Emotions

Author: Deepti Dogra

First published in 2021 by Think Tank Books™, New Delhi

Address: RZ-26/27B, Ashok Park, West Sagarpur, New Delhi - 110046

Website: thinktankbooks.com

Email: editorial@thinktankbooks.com

Printed at: Thomson Press
18/35 Delhi-Mathura Road, Faridabad, Haryana 121007

ISBN: 978-81-947561-8-7

Price: INR 165/-

Maximum retail price of this book listed is only for the Indian subcontinent. Selling price may vary elsewhere.

5 4 3 2 1

*Dedicated to all those who search for
companionship within themselves.*

~~~Contents~~~
~~~

~~~Acknowledgements~~~

Many different feelings and emotions over the years and penning them down has motivated me to give it the shape of my first poetry book. It is not a destination but a humble beginning and manifestation for aspiring to be an author. Each poem is a true expression of my inside world and gave me immense joy in writing.

I would first like to acknowledge the motivation of Dr. Ravi K Dhar, Professor and Director of JIMS, Vasant Kunj, and also my teacher in the college for appreciating all my poems, style, and content as well as encouraging me to proceed for publishing this book, The Madness of Emotions.

I am grateful to my parents, Dr. Satish Kumar Dogra and Ms. Sharda Dogra who have always been there for me in thick and thin. Their motivation and support has immensely helped me in this literary venture.

A final special mention to the whole team of Think Tank Books, especially Mr. Gaurav Sharma, Alma Mater of JIMS who has helped in the execution of the book in the final form.

~~~About the Author~~~

Deepti Dogra is a freelance content writer as well as a lifestyle and fashion blogger. Born in 1993 in Chandigarh, she is an avid reader and loves to write. She also has a huge interest in makeup artistry. She has been writing poetry since the age of 15 and has always wanted to be a published author.

A graduate in Journalism and Mass Communication from JIMS, IP University, she loves to travel, try different cuisines, and is always active on social media.

Deepti loves to express her feelings through poetry and other ways of writing and always keeps a small diary with herself to write down if the creative juices flow in.

Residing in Vasant Kunj, you will often find her at a café with a book along with her. This is her debut book and she is preparing to make this a successful full-time career. You can always connect with her on Instagram @ deeptidogramua.

~~~Existence~~~

Lost and found
My existence is not yet essential
Without my life's purpose
I don't feel any more valuable

They say it's going to work out
Things will get better soon
Then why don't I see a ray of hope
The rise of that sunshine

I do believe I deserve better
But better might not think so
I want a happy ending
But not in such a slow-mo

~~~**Dear Lover**~~~

Love me please
Even when I hate you
Never ask me to leave
You know my real problems

I know I will be difficult
At times,
A stone under your feet
But don't throw away me please
You know my real problems

Don't give me the silent treatment
In frustration,
Don't forget me for someone else
Please wait, I still love you
Even if I say I don't
You know my real problems

Love me please
When I'm a thunder
You did love me
When I was a sunrise

~~~Never Let You Go~~~

Maybe there's a way to walk away
Maybe there will be a happy day
Or maybe I can close my eyes
And make these troubles go away

There's a flicker of light
In this dark room
Called happiness
And I'm going to let it bloom

I refuse to turn back
And leave you scared and alone
I'll always hold your hand
And no matter what
Never let you go

I see the thunderstorm glaring
As if warning us to let go of each other
But aren't our vows stronger
Than a timed dilemma

So close your eyes
For I'm going to be the way now
To over the top euphoria
Because isn't it obvious
I'll never let you go

~~~The Other Side~~~

I got a side of me
Dark to the blind
A part of me
Silent for the loud
You may call it a mood swing
But it's a white halcyon wing

Serendipity lead me
To my esoteric reality
And as lonely as it may seem
I already feel being crowded
By a world sitting back
To tag me as a loner

I look soft as cotton
A pushover ready for taunts and comments
No one would deem me
To be as hard as a rock
Swift like the wind
My own knight

This rare side of me
Is a painted sea
Of the waves rushing over the sand
Would it be wrong if I
Give in to the waves finally
And put myself at ease

~~~When You Least Expect~~~

All ways have been the same
In the storming waves of my forest
I've shed blood unwantedly
And usually wantedly
Hoping to catch an eye
Thinking it can make a difference

First love is a new high
A permanent addiction for life
First heartbreak seems a new picture
Making you believe
You know how the world runs

You know the ups and downs
The highs and lows
You do miss her voice
Tingling in your ears
But you man up and swallow
What's left of your confused emotions

And although you may not believe
But this isn't the part that hurts the most
This isn't the turmoil that takes away everything
Following are worse life lessons
Waiting to punch you in the stomach
When you least expect

~~~First Love~~~

Is it just me
Or you feel the same
When we lay eyes on each other
The butterflies in the stomach
The violins in the background
Wishing no one else was around

The sparks when you touch my hand
Have lit up a fire inside me
All I want to know
Has it burnt your heart as well

I try but can't stop
Writing about your endless beauty
Your captive fragrance
Your kohl eyed glances

Our silences make enough noise
As we stare at the starry night sky
Declaring our goals and dreams
Somehow holding our hands in between

~~~My Bloody Mess~~~

Holding the sharpest thorns
Of my wild rose
I bleed unknowingly
With open wounds on my soul

Like a child I believed
For someone to aid me
And yet here I am
Cleaning my own bloody mess

One cut here, one bruise there
Yet I only blame myself
For waiting so long down that rainy road
For all the solutions, all the help
That never existed

~~~There was a Time~~~

There was a time
When love was a crime
There was a time
When solitude seemed right

I don't recall meeting you
When everything else turned into fumes
And all I was left with
Was loving you

You became my home
The one I surrendered to
The only one I could see
My future with

Yet here I am
Without you, without any goodbyes
Again in the silence of seclusion
But much happier than in the lies before

At least my confinement makes me free
With no ugly demands
But a memory
That there was a time
When I had fallen for someone

~~~The Truth~~~

As the lights go out
Every night
I hear the sound of music
The same masterpiece
For it covers a bigger truth

A truth that often leaves scars
A truth known by all
But spoken by none
A truth which needs to be stopped

It first pains you
And then apologises
It, who can't be called human
It, who has been carrying on this ritual
It, who needs to feel the same

And she left with no respect or love
But wounds on her body and heart
Scared and petrified
She doesn't really belong here
In a made up house of hell

But she's made to believe
She's too weak
To stand up to the real world
To live on her own terms
To be a real woman

While some get the chance
To reborn when they can
Many of them let that opportunity go
For the sake of others' respect
Unknowingly choosing self-torture

~~~If I Could Go Back~~~

If I could go back to myself
To my mistakes and failures
To stop the biggest blunders
I will have to say no

If could get a chance
To be the old me
To find my innocence again
I'll have to say no

I'll pass the three wishes
That take me to the past
The three wishes
That may change the way I am

Sure, I've been hurt a million times
In a million ways
Have been told a variety of lies
Almost every day

I've been cheated countlessly
For I was the naïve one
But never did I regret
For choosing the wrong person

Those are the mistakes
That have built me up
Those are the failures
That have taught me about success

I may make many more
As you might know
To err is human
But if I could go back
To change all that
I would always say no

~~~Mirror~~~

Staring into the mirror
I see a girl looking back at me
Confused, hurt and decorated
She looks nothing like me

A fake reflection
And yet loved by all
My true self
Hides somewhere in me

She's beautiful
She's exaggerated
Because she's wanted by all
And groomed for all

But she's not me
Her hair, her face
Her injected lips
Are no longer recognised by me
In the mirror

~~~Once Upon a Time~~~

Why has love erupted
New meanings every day
Why has it taken over
Temporary relationships
Where all promise a forever

Why has love become a lie
A lie that all want to believe
Often seeming like a relief
But are scared of it
Turning into a heartbreak

Once upon a time
Love was known as pure
True and unadulterated
Today, it has been left
As just a word

Transformed into lust
It usually stays with you for a night
And the morning after
Is only left for an awkward goodbye

~~~**Moments**~~~

There were moments to cry for
Moments to die for
Moments that made me feel
I'm the one you're made for

Hopelessly and blindly
I gave you all the love I had
Imagined a future together
Even though I knew it's a blunder

I cried on your shoulder
Smiled in your arms
And yet couldn't decode you
You were never mine

I've cried in shower
Thinking of our memory lane
I've worn my sadness
Like a queen's crown

I won't forget
Those moments we shared
But you're in the past for me
And the past needs to go

~~~Sun of Hope~~~

In the ice cold street
I keep moving with my bare feet
With no one to hold my hand
No one to give me some burning heat

I often fall as I get tired
I often feel empty inside
It's seldom that this seems a phase
For there are always new problems to face

And yet my sun of hope never died
Possibly will never do
Although I've cried enough times
Hoping the next time I won't do

There's more than hope in me
Whispering in my ear
That as the seasons change
My time will do as well

And sure, problems will come and go
But there's a silver lining to every cloud
A positive built to every negative crowd
Now it's up to me what I see
It's up to me what I believe

~~~The Last Time~~~

Trapped in an unlocked cage
I'm too afraid to step out
Captured by my fears
I'm too coward to be bold

I feel lost inside myself
Disabled to take a step without falling
Uncomfortable in my own skin
A body without a soul

I can barely recall
The last time I felt normal
The last time I was happy
The last time I could talk

They say
Silence can speak a thousand words
Yet mine chooses to be useless
As I absorb everything inside

And even when I want to speak
I lose my words
I know my story
But can't let it out to others

~~~Beginning of the End~~~

Why are you looking for answers
Of the questions never asked
Trying to make this
A fair world
When unfairness can only last

Every time you thought
You had found a fair deal
Someone would wake you up
To let you know it's just a dream

All those happy endings
And perfect love stories
Look better placed in the books
For reality never made space for them

Labelled by the world
Once you have stepped out
It's never easy to get your character assassinated
For the choices you've made

And when being pointed at
Laughed at
When you need all that support
You find yourself alone
Covering your mouth with a pillow
As the tears make you fall apart

You hope it would end
Like a nightmare
You hope to make amends
You wish you had friends
Unfortunately,
It's only the beginning of the end

~~~**Bloody Family**~~~

I found a way to cope up
The day I woke up
I didn't know what to say
But I knew I would find a way

What's left to do is not for you
I no longer need your say
No I don't need your approval
It's either my way or the high way

I've heard enough lies
And enough apologies
So what if we're related
It didn't stop you from being abusive

While I got scarred
You lived in denial
Called it your love
Called it being parental

And now when I've got nothing for you
No feelings, not even hate
You beg to be in my life
You claim we share the same blood
But what about the time
When you were ready to shed it

The world is lending me its advice
Family will always be by your side
They gave you birth, how can you be so cruel
Commenting on my lifestyle, my conduct
When they haven't lived a day of my life

I don't believe that the past can be forgotten
At least not all of it
For the past is the foundation of the future
For my past is what I am today
And what I will be tomorrow

~~~Future~~~

Stories can be lies
Respect can be an impression
Glorious devotion can be means
To prove a non-existing love
To make you believe in it

As auspicious as it sounds
The love in the air has been polluted
Falling in it is no longer wanted
Love is only a mind game now
Based on lust and greed

I rarely see a couple
Still wanting to grow old together
But when I do
I see a hope
True love may still exist

I see a future
Where the next generations
Don't talk about love
As history

I see a future
Where love doesn't bring tears
In its hidden pocket

I see a future
Where broken hearts
Can be mended forever

~~~Hold On~~~

There's a rush
With some pain
There are tears
In the rain
In our era called life

You will see vows
Often being broken
Happy laughter and smile
Hiding a bigger sadness
Holding on to a thread of hope
From a mountain of denial

Peaceful summer fields
To breathe in the fresh air
Healing your hidden pain
And your pillow tears

Even on that tiny thread
Hold on
For a future lay ahead
Don't think that it would break
Just imagine it turning it big

~~~Not Everyone~~~

Not everyone conquers the world
Not everyone has to be at the top
You do what you want to
You do what you love
Don't just become another money worshiper
Don't just think about big bucks

The competition will begin the minute you're born
And your future will be decided then and there
Don't be surprised if your opinion is not asked
It's a tradition to force a broken dream on the child

But don't kill the artist inside you
By going for engineering
Don't throw away that guitar
To become a corporate slave

Don't fulfil their aspirations
Only to hate yourself later
Don't try to find job satisfaction
In something you hate
Work on something you've always loved
And the money and satisfaction will creep in later

~~~Be My Best Friend~~~

You make me fall in love
And then you say goodbye
You proclaim it as a place of heaven
But hell it is, I soon realise

Confusion dissolves the truth
Is this something I was trying to find
Or a phase of life
Better to avoid

When you're closer than my soul
I lose my breath
And in a moment of truth
You're gone like a ghost

I forget myself in your presence
And I call it a criminal offence
I left you to do myself a favour
To be my best friend
To add some flavour

You reap what you sow
And if one day
You want me back
I would give my everything
To say no

~~~Dead or Alive~~~

I search for a look in your eyes
That I'm unable to define
Those positive vibes
Have attracted me for a while

I have looked for you
In my dreams all night
My search for you
Now seems like a fight

I often feel your presence
Somewhere around
An unfamiliar but homely essence
Like you're about to be found

But suddenly it all disappears
Much before I can come out of its illusion
Bringing me back to my prayers
Back to My Old Life

Either my imagination has gone wild
Or your existence is absolute
Either I am dead
Or you're not alive

~~~A Phase or Not~~~

It's been here for a long time
It's been tied up to my soul
It feels like home to me
And yet I want it to go away
It has set camp in my body
And stopped everything in its way

I can breathe and yet feel dead
I want to scream
But I am voiceless
I no longer find any reason to smile
I have no reason and yet I cry

I often look around
Trying to find its cause
I often pretend
Like nothing's wrong
But feel more than lonely
When in a crowd

I've been told
It's just a phase
You should go out more
And it will go away

But I feel it tightening on me
Its touch making me lethargic
I panic when I think
Of the future lay ahead

Will I be the same droopy sad girl
Feeling dead inside
Or will I be someone normal
Someone happy

~~~The Mirage~~~

I feel safe
I feel loved
I feel like home
Often when I think about you

But I feel threatened
I feel hated
I feel scared
When I see you

This love is a mirage
A reflection of me
Screening only
What I want to see

This love is a bubble
It may burst anytime
Break all the dreams
And lay the truth in no time

I no longer trust you
Follow you around
To find if you are what you say
Or you are the other way around

It has pained me more than enough
To be with you
To be scarred by you
To think it was right
To still be with you

My days are spent in hope
To be your love
And not just a need
While my nights are spent in tears
That this is just a waste of me
And my time

~~~**You Were Dead**~~~

I fell on the ground
Ached for you
Felt your need
Called you out
But didn't see you around

In the hazy winter morning
I saw you leaving me
I screamed your name
Again and again
Why didn't you pay any heed

Torn into pieces
With a broken heart
I saw a white light
Falling upon

As you disappear with a smile
Our goodbye are endless
And I finally realize
That all this while
You were dead

~~~Deep Waters~~~

Why remorse
Over the bygones
Who never treasured you

> Why be aimless
> And saddened
> By self-proclaimed lovers

> > These are deep waters
> > That you are drowning in
> > Searching for what doesn't exists

Killing yourself
Piece by piece
As you unknowingly
Fall in the arms of
Another fake lover

~~~Love Arrangements~~~

It felt like a dream
Or perhaps a nightmare
With someone sitting beside me
To be my forever

It changed my life
As the sunshine transformed into a shimmering
darkness
Loaded with unknown duties
Every step of mine whiffed of nervousness

Man and wife
But strangers till date
He didn't know I drink
I didn't know he could bake

Hesitant and awkward
We were far from adjusting as a couple
I could take his surname for sure
But wasn't allowed to know home before

Years and years later
And after a gazillion trial runs
We still couldn't magically complete each other's
sentences

But after umpteenth of irrational fights
We surely knew each other
Better than ourselves

~~~Complicated~~~

As the moonlight fell on her face
Her skin glowed more than ever
The white gown shimmered in the night sky
Making her smile twinkle like the stars

That day was no ordinary
For it was changing him
To become a better person
Perfectly suited as the groom
He waited at the altar
For his dream girl to become his wife

They had vowed to be loyal
A best friend to each other
And the love of their lives
Till the day they died

No rules were involved
No games no poker face
It was so rare for a couple to know
And to understand
That since ages love had never been complicated
For people were the ones
Adding the complications

~~~Waiting~~~

I wouldn't have minded waiting
If your feelings were so indefinite
I would have waited for you
If you weren't so distant

Why were all your decisions
Inclusive of all this distance
The more I tried to come
The further you ran away

I always thought
That one day you'll be back
Back to take my hand
Back to be my man

But I soon realized
That day would only be a dream
And why should I pain myself
By waiting for a dead end

~~~Fierce Obsession~~~

She was his bread and butter
Wanted to keep her under his hands
His stalking skills had levelled higher
Perhaps leading to something bad

She belongs to me
The thought always ran through his mind
While she had no idea
About her oncoming fate

He loved her eyes
The spark in them
He was always around
Looking out for them

The day finally came
When he asked her out
When a random guy confessed his love
To a girl who didn't have a clue about his existence

Brought her favourite flowers
Recited her beloved poem
But to his shock
Was humiliated in front of many

It was an unforgettable nightmare
How could she do this to him
He would always ask
His love had turned into fire
He wanted his avenge

He recalled her eyes
Those shiny ones
That spark was soon gone
Once he washed them with acid

~~~Unnatural Love~~~

Our love is no different
Our love is not bad
So what if I love a woman
So what if I don't prefer a man

They call it a mental disorder
Some say it's a trending lifestyle
I say I was born with it
You can call it the God's style

It was confusing at first
When I thought I was the only one
Who had a crush on a girl
Never gossiped about boys

But it felt like home
And it felt right
I never felt impure
I never found it unnatural

And why is it wrong
To marry the one you really love
Instead of getting hitched
Somewhere I don't belong

~~~Little Dreams~~~

Encircle inside boundaries
And unfair rules
I still pray to the Almighty
Hoping for some good news

I don't recall the time
When I started here
But I do know I'd been through a lot
As an infant without any care

My day begins with
Carrying hot cups of tea
But none of them are for me
Cleaning tables in and out
Wearing rugged torn clothes
That weren't even bought

I often see kids of my age
In blue shirts and grey pants
Leaving for school
With loaded bags

It's a beautiful sight
Like a starry night sky
I wish to be a part of them
Studying those books

Opening locked doors
Creating a new life

I pray to all the Gods
Of all the religions
To give me that chance
To make a life for once
That isn't what others demand

~~~Be The Person~~~

Strong and independent
She had learned from her mistakes
Expensive gifts were not her thing
Her belief was earning her diamonds

Long nights at work had paid immensely
And success had made its way to her
The now proud parents
Never missed a chance to praise their daughter

An inspiration to all classes of women
Often mentoring them up the lane
Her face was always supposed to beam like a pretty
thing
Even when her heart felt brittle

The winner stands alone
The saying was completely true
Millions of followers around
Dying to get a picture with her
But none to share her stardom

Isolated and exhausted
She gathered her courage everyday
To be the person they all expected
To be what she was known for

~~~The Trophy Wife~~~

Diamonds for her birthday
And vacations to every other place
She lived an envious life
But the truth was something else

I won't be able to make it today
Was her husband's excuse for the day
Even on their wedding anniversary date

Instead, expensive gifts replaced his presence
And the love she longed for
Ended up at the city's designer stores

Her marriage was like a reality show
He believed in sex, not love
He believed in many, not one

His affairs with younger women were out of the
bag
Everyone knew and yet pretended to be blind
And while she could choose infidelity too
She just didn't want to go that low

When out with him
They would smile and kiss
Act like an adorable couple

But for him
She was only a trophy wife

~~~Not a Wife~~~

Coffee served hot
With a few biscuits by the side
It was all they could afford
To showcase their daughter

She wore no diamonds
And no gold chains
Her treasure was something better
Her love for knowledge
And its everlasting power

The starboy paid no heed to it
After all, he was the breadwinner
Lusting for a wishful dowry
Not an educated wife

They all looked at her
like customers in a furniture store
While commenting on her dark skin tone
Said he wouldn't mind the colour
But the college degrees would have to go

As a wife she served his parents during the day
And had to become his slave for the night
Often unwillingly
When isolation accompanied with tears

She realized that he needed a maid
and an escort
Not a wife

~~~That Game Called Life~~~

Scarred for life
She had a deal with fear
Open or closed
Her eyes were always filled with tears
She had accepted her fate
Whatever came her way
To be her destiny
No matter with how much hate

Often looking out of the window
She tried to find reasons
Reasons for the painful wounds
Given by those she had trusted
Those who were family

Maturity stroke to let her know the fact
That life didn't run on rules
It was an unfair game
Seeking opportunities to pull you back

But Karma had a nasty menu
Doesn't matter if you order or not
It would always serve what you deserve

~~~A Pit of Depression~~~

I breathe fire in and out
And yet I don't burn down
Lonely and absorbing darkness
I don't understand this feeling somehow
Where even with a dozen people around
I feel like falling into a pit

I often cry myself to sleep
But it never makes me feel any better
I'm sad, I believe
But why? I don't understand

Those people I loved
And could die for
All those feelings have disappeared
All my love is lost

Avoiding friend by saying I'm busy
Cancelling on parties
I feed on loneliness
And yet I want to talk to someone

I stopped taking care of myself a long time ago
No showers for days
With greasy hair on the go
I feel like a dead body

Maybe I need help
Like a medicine for fever
Because no longer do I feel content
And sorrow is my follower

~~~If it Matters~~~

If it matters to you
Then make it work
If it matters to you
Then the excuses should stop
If it matters you
Then take a stand for it

You might be innocent in nature
But it won't let you drag someone else's limits
Those limits that once she was ready to drag herself
She gave you power over her
But she can immediately take it back

Don't find her submissive
Standing there taking your assaults
She respects you
But her dignity has always been a priority

Playing with her feelings
And apologizing every time won't work
You've crossed every limit
No expectations is what you said
So follow the same as well

~~~Made a Wish~~~

I made a wish on Christmas
To let you know I exist
Making the Clause do all the work

But as the days got old
I saw no changes unfold
You were the school's John Stamos
And I was Little Miss Unknown

Then came my birthday
And again I made a wish to be with you
For you to be my first and last
For you to never be in my past

And then came a day
You caught me out of the blue
To be your date
For the dance next week

Shrieking in excitement
I shopped for the perfect shoes and dress
I was going with Mr. Perfect after all
I had to look my best

At the night of the dance
I nervously waited

For you to pick me up
Hours passed by
And you were nowhere to be found
Reality hit me hard
Paining as I realized that I had been a joke
A possible dare
Who you must be laughing about

My dark night didn't
Witness my tears
Because I had become a laughingstock
But I'd realized
That perfection didn't come from
Glossy hair, big built and popularity

~~~Piece of Pleasure~~~

Dressed in red
And made up to look her best
She was told to stay silent
Till it got over

Unaware of her future
She did what was told
It's the best for her, they said
Becoming the bride
Of someone so old

The scary old man
Had a toothless smile
And as she was handed over to him
The daughter began crying

The mother remained silent
Letting her child go away
Where?
Even she didn't know

Recalling her painful wedding night
When her childish screams were heard by no one
She knew her daughter would have the same fate

They were nothing but a piece of pleasure
To be used as needed

~~~The Forgotten Courtesan~~~

Standing in the summer breeze
The unfaithful sand
And the seasonal heat
I once again waited for a sign
For you to reveal yourself

And every day I waited
Till the moonlight showed up
Struggling with a hope
To see you one day

Years have passed
Since you promised to come back
Since you asked me to wait
Since I let my womanhood surpass

And I often let myself ponder
Do you even remember me?
Or my name?
Perhaps you have a family
With a lovely wife
Children in a suburban house

And me?
I'm just a mistake
A night of passion

Who is long forgotten
After all,
Who remembers a courtesan?

~~~Story of a Damsel~~~

Till this day
I remember that night
The darkness had blended
It was time to say goodbye

Believe me when I disclose
I never wanted to let you go
Alas, you were a part of me
My blood and soul

Sentenced for my blunder
Hatred was spread for an angel
Death was the ultimate order
Because you were a damsel

I pleaded and cried
Begged for mercy
Offered them my life
To save my progeny

But my child
Was solely a liability
And her birth a crime
Snatched from my arms
She was abolished
At the first chance

~~~The Closet~~~

What love was to him
Seemed unconditionally
Unnatural to them
It was only proposed
For a man and a woman

He had often discovered
Opinions of the powerful
It's a disease
It's a hobby
It's a phase
Solely he knew
That none of it was true

The closet was quite cramped for him
There were so many with their squirm
Acceptance was the real struggle
Whether by himself
Or the masses

He had been called names
Like feminine
But he looked no less than a man
So what gave out?
He often asked

In love
He would always choose
The Bachelor over Pretty Woman
Finding 'the one' wasn't a concern
Leaving the closet was

~~~Sea of the Living~~~

It's a sea out there
Once you start to live
You find yourself flowing
Regardless of what you think

What you want today
Will surely not be needed later
The love you desire today
Might be an infatuation in the near future

There are times when you feel dead
Even as you take in the mountain air
Hopelessness may take over
Even as you step out of despair

However,
Trust me when I convey
This is the life
Most of you may abide
And the rest would survive

<center>~~~You~~~</center>

As the moon shines
On your face I realize
I've been waiting for you
All my life

When you hold my hand
And kiss me on the forehead
I feel so loved
It feels so right

Walking by your side
When I look at you
And you kiss me
You sweep me off my feet

I smile as I realize my luck
That I ended up with you
For you
By you

My hope lasts forever
But even if we don't
I will always remain in love
With you

***